The Adventures of Spike and Prickles

Thank you...

I would like to take this opportunity to thank all the lovely people who have helped make this book happen.

My children for constantly encouraging me to write down the bedtime stories I told them all those years ago.

Family and friends who gave open and honest feedback on the early drafts.

Grace Dowley for well needed early guidance and corrections, so appreciated.

Rose Skelton for bringing to life my imagination.
Your illustrations are fantastic and thank you for your patience in accommodating my 'fine tuning'.

Ann Newman for spending endless hours correcting and improving the flow, grammar and adding the descriptive colour that was definitely missing.

Humphrey Keenlyside for his excellent proof reading, ensuring all the i's were dotted and t's were crossed.

Finally, Chris Witham, my lifelong friend and newly found publisher, for his invaluable guidance and support in helping make this happen. I have thoroughly enjoyed every minute of the journey and without you, 'The Adventures of Spike and Prickles' would still be gathering dust on my computer's hard drive for many years to come.

Martin Somers 2021

Book One

A Forest Divided

Written by
Martin Somers

Illustrated by
Rose Skelton

Contents

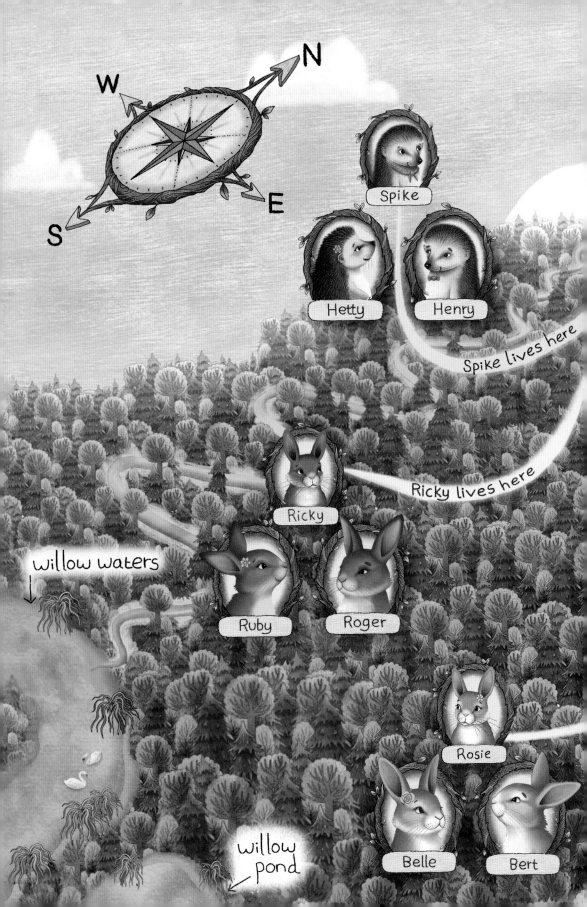

N

W

E

S

Spike

Hetty

Henry

Spike lives here

Ricky

Ricky lives here

willow waters

Ruby

Roger

Rosie

willow pond

Belle

Bert

Hill Top

Hollow pond

Prickles

Pippa

Pop

Prickles lives here

Short Hill

Sami and Stan live here

Rosie lives here

Sami

Stan

Safi

Syd

Oakwood Forest

Chapter One

The Great Storm

Prickles was petrified and every spine on her back was trembling. The storm her father had predicted arrived faster than expected and she was holding on to her mother in fear for her life. She could hear the rain crashing down on the ground above, the wind howling in anger and constant cracks of thunder, which followed huge bolts of lightning, so bright they even managed to light up their burrow, which was beneath a holly bush.

Her fear got worse, as every minute the storm appeared to intensify, and she started to worry that their normally safe and warm home wouldn't protect the three of them from the terrifying noises she could hear up above.

"Will we be okay, Dad?" she asked in a trembling voice.
"Of course, we will, my little one," he replied.

She could tell he was worried and had heard him say to her mother earlier, "This storm looks like it's going to be a bad one. I have never seen it get so dark so quickly or seen the wind pick up so fast. Let's hope our home will withstand it!"

Prickles sat there trembling as she held her mother tighter than ever and then started to worry about Spike, her best friend.

Only an hour ago she had been playing her favourite game of hide and seek around the Great Oak Tree with Spike and her other friends, Rosie and Ricky, two bouncy young rabbits, and Sami and Stanley (Stan for short), two superfast young twin squirrels.

They were playing near the Great Oak Tree without a care in the world and she was singing her favourite song:

> Hide and seek is so much fun
> I'll soon find you one by one
> I will look under roots and behind the trees
> There is no way you're hiding from me.

Suddenly her father, Pop, appeared and came rushing up to them. "You need to get back to your homes as fast as you can," he said, panting. "There's a storm coming, and it looks like it could be a big one. Get inside and don't come out until it's passed."

The friends could hear the concern in his voice and ran as fast they could back to the safety of their homes.

Prickles and Pop did the same.

Prickles was worried about Spike, as it was much further to his home at Hilltop than her house.

"Dad, do you think Spike got back in time?" she asked in a worried voice. "Of course, he did my little one," he replied. "That youngster is the fastest hedgehog I've ever seen."

This made Prickles much happier, but she still held on to her mother as tightly as she possibly could, squeezing in closer every time there was another mighty crack of thunder.

Prickles started thinking about her friends. She was born just over a year ago. Her best friend was Spike, who was born the week before her. Both her parents, Pippa and Pop, and Spike's parents, Hetty and Henry, had always been friends. She had spent every day of her short life playing and exploring with Spike. They only met Rosie, Ricky, Sami and Stan more recently, when playing hide and seek around the Great Oak Tree.

The rabbits, Rosie and Ricky, had wandered up and asked if they could join in and play the game too. As playing hide and seek is so much fun with more animals, the hedgehogs were delighted that they wanted to join their game and welcomed them with open arms. Rosie and Ricky were also best friends and lived with their parents in an area of Oakwood Forest called Westwood, which wasn't far away and close to where Spike and his parents lived.

A few weeks after they had met Rosie and Ricky, things got even better when the twin squirrels, Sami and Stan, appeared and asked if they, too, could join in the game. They were out jumping high up in the trees when Stan, saw the hedgehogs and rabbits playing together.

The squirrels went and introduced themselves, asking if they could also join in the game. From that day on, the six of them became inseparable, playing and exploring together, meeting every morning at the Great Oak Tree. The twin squirrels also lived with their parents in an area of the forest called Eastwood, close to Prickles home.

Another loud crack of thunder made Prickles jump. The storm seemed to grow in strength, and she couldn't help fearing the worst, especially when water started coming down the steps into the burrow. It was obvious that they couldn't go outside because they wouldn't survive the torrential rain, howling winds, falling branches and bolts of lightning bombarding their beloved forest. However, staying inside meant they faced the risk of drowning if the burrow filled up with water.

As always, Pop quickly took control and moved things around in the burrow, so they had a wide shelf to rest on, keeping them well above the water that had started to flow in. Pippa explained that if the water did reach the shelf, they would have to leave their home and make their way to the old rabbit burrow underneath the Great Oak Tree. Prickles knew this well as she often used its entrance as a hiding place. It would be dangerous, but probably their only option.

Prickles loved the way her mother and father worked together as a team and knew they were both putting on a brave face for her. Despite the constant noises and the ever-rising water, she somehow managed to fall asleep, still clutching her mother tightly.

Suddenly, she was woken by a massive crash that was louder than the thunder and shook the ground so hard, it made her fall off the shelf and into the water.

Prickles found herself panicking and spluttering at the shock of being woken by both the crash and falling into the water. As she waved her arms frantically to keep her head above the rising pool, Pippa quickly leaned in to grab her, with Pop holding firmly onto Pippa's rear legs so she didn't fall in too. Pippa pulled her back onto the shelf, calming her down as she coughed and spluttered having swallowed lots of water.

"What was that?" she cried. "Did you hear it? Did you feel it?"
"Yes, yes," said her parents at the same time, looking at each other to see if the other one had any idea what had caused the loud crashing noise which had literally made the earth shake.

The hedgehogs huddled on the shelf together, with Pippa wrapping Prickles in a blanket to help her keep warm. They were questioning each other on what could have caused the massive crash when suddenly Pop said, "Shush, listen."

They immediately fell into silence and soon realised that the noises from the storm, that had kept them awake and fearing for their lives throughout the night, had finally stopped.

Prickles was so relieved that they had survived the storm, but she was desperately worried about her friends and the damage to their beloved forest.

She couldn't hold in her emotions any more and started to cry, thinking about Spike and his parents.

When she looked at the pool of water that had filled their home, she worried if the same, or possibly worse, could have happened to them.

By early morning the rain had stopped, and, as it had been some time since they heard either the storm or falling branches, Pop decided it was safe enough to venture out and inspect the damage.
Prickles' parents went slightly ahead to clear the debris that was blocking the entrance to their home.

As they stepped out into the early morning sunshine, they held paws and just stood in silence, looking at all the fallen trees, broken branches and crushed bushes that were all around them.

They were there for a few minutes, when suddenly Prickles thought about Spike and rushed off shouting behind her, "I must see if Spike is okay," and went running as fast as she could towards the Great Oak Tree. Prickles suddenly stopped in her tracks and stood there frozen, her mouth wide open in shock.

Chapter Two

The King of
Oakwood Forest falls

Prickles stood there in disbelief at what she saw. She didn't know whether to laugh or cry. All her friends, Spike, Rosie, Ricky, Sami and Stan, were there in front of her, safe and holding paws with their parents, which made her so happy, but they all had their heads down in sadness. They were looking at the Great Oak Tree, but instead of it standing proud, like the king of the forest, it was lying on the ground, its immense trunk flattening many smaller trees and bushes.

Prickles not only lived near the Great Oak Tree, but spent every day playing around it with her forest friends and having dinner every evening with all the families. The sadness of its loss and all the emotions from the previous night were too much for her and the tears started flow.

Spike was staring at the fallen Great Oak Tree, also thinking about how lucky they had been to survive a storm so intense that it even brought down the king of the forest. He was just about to go and see if Prickles and her parents were safe, when he sensed her behind him and turned around to see her standing there with tears running down her face.

He rushed up and held her close, letting her cry whilst neither of them said a word. The others watched them in silence, with tears of happiness, relieved that they survived the great storm, but sad at the destruction it had caused, especially the loss of the Great Oak Tree.

After a little while, they all came together and sat around in a circle to talk about what had happened. All the other adults thanked Pop for raising the alarm and sending the youngsters home, but at the same time questioning how he knew the storm was coming.

"I've seen the signs before," Pop said. "A sky darkening so quickly and a sudden increase in wind usually means a storm is coming, but I've never seen one come so quickly or one so strong. We were very lucky!"

They nodded in agreement and each of them took turns to describe the events of the night.

It was clear that Prickles, Pop and Pippa had the worst experience, especially with their burrow filling with water. It also became clear that the Great Oak Tree crashing to the ground was the cause of the massive shock wave that resulted in Prickles falling into the water. The adult squirrels, Saffi and Syd, told the others how they had also feared for their lives, with the trees swaying so much in the howling wind they thought the trunk of the tree that was their home would snap.

They decided it would be safer underground and ended up spending the night in an old rabbit burrow at the base of another oak tree. Fortunately, the tree sheltered the burrow from the worst of the rain, so it was dry enough to sleep in.

As the weeks passed, life in the forest slowly returned to normal. It was now late spring and, despite all the damage caused by the storm, Oakwood Forest was looking and sounding beautiful again. The trees were full of fresh new green leaves, the birds were singing the most wonderful tunes and fresh smells were oozing from the ground as the sun rose and dried the dew off the forest floor.

Every morning, the youngsters would meet at the fallen Great Oak Tree to play their games, while the adults went in search of food. Everyone gathered at lunch and dinner time to enjoy delicious feasts of nuts, grass and insects, while talking about the adventures of the day.

Between meals, the youngsters would be either playing or exploring. Spike was a natural explorer and always wanted to discover new areas of the forest, whereas Prickles was a creator, who loved making up games and songs for everyone to play and sing. Her favourite game was hide and seek, which they all loved, especially now with all the fallen trees and holes in the ground from the uprooted trunks providing so many new places to hide.

They took it in turns to do the seeking, while the others hid, always singing the song that Prickles had made up:

Hide and seek is so much fun
I'll soon find you one by one
I will look under roots and behind the trees
There is no way you're hiding from me.

The animals had given names to different parts of the forest, which helped when they were talking about things they had seen, or different areas they had visited. Sami and Stan lived in an area called Eastwood, where the sun rose each morning, while Rosie and Ricky lived in an area called Westwood, where the sun set in the evening. The area the sun crossed during the day was called Southwood and opposite this was Northwood.

Prickles and her parents lived right in the centre of Oakwood Forest, which was always referred to as Oakwood because of the Great Oak Tree. Spike lived in a higher area called Hilltop, which was between Westwood and Northwood.

One beautiful morning, the sun was shining, birds were singing, and the friends met as usual by the fallen Great Oak Tree.

"Morning everyone," said Spike, who was usually the last to arrive, mainly because he had the longest journey to reach Oakwood from Hilltop. "Shall we go exploring today?" he said with excitement.

"On the way here, I bumped into my friends, Daisy and Dexter, the deer. They told me about a great area they had found in Eastwood," Spike went on. "They said it has a big slope like the ones around Hilltop, but instead of it going all the way to the bottom, it flattens out, so you can race down it and only have a short hill to climb back up. This means we could have many short races, without getting too tired walking back up. Sounds like fun to me. What do you think?"

They were all nodding and clapping with excitement, and quickly went to tell their parents where they were going.

After being told to be careful, especially of foxes and badgers, and to make sure they collected food on the way for lunch and to be back just before sunset in time for dinner, they set off with a spring in their step and not a care in the world.

Prickles made up a song to pass away the time during their journey:

We're going somewhere we've never been before
Good old Spike he loves to explore
We're going to Eastwood to find the short hill
Let's hope the races give us a thrill.

It didn't take long before the six of them were singing the song and by mid-morning they had reached the short hill, having stopped for a short rest on the way and to collect some food for lunch.

The short hill was very similar to Hilltop, but instead of the slope going all the way to the bottom, one side of the hill flattened out halfway down, which meant they had plenty of time to stop.

What made it even more special was that there were only a few trees and bushes, so you could run down any part of it without worrying about hitting an obstacle.

"Let's race to the bottom," shouted Sami in excitement, and without waiting for the others to agree, he was off, speeding down the steep slope as fast as his little squirrel legs would take him. Stan, Rosie and Ricky were annoyed with Sami, who was always misbehaving and went running after him, but no one stood a chance of catching him.

They reached the bottom and Stan was just about to tell his brother off for cheating and getting a head start, when Sami looked back up the slope and started laughing. They all turned and looked up only to see poor Spike and Prickles, whose little legs were struggling to keep up as they tried to run down the steep slope. By the time they reached the bottom, both the hedgehogs were exhausted and furious that Sami had been laughing at them all the way, especially as he had also cheated.

"That's not fair," shouted Spike, "we can't run as fast as you."

"Not my problem," said Sami. "Anyway, it was your idea to come here, not ours."

Spike was angry that he and Prickles couldn't match the others for speed. Prickles went over to give him a hug and whispered in his ear, "Don't worry, Spike, I've got a plan."

Prickles turned to Sami and said, "Spike and I could beat you easily. We just didn't try."

"No, you couldn't," Sami replied confidently. "Even if we gave you a ten-second start you couldn't beat any of us. I'll even bet my lunch on it!"

Spike was scratching his head, wondering why Prickles thought two slow hedgehogs could ever beat squirrels or rabbits, but knew she had never let him down in the past, so decided to stay quiet and go along with her plan.

"Okay," said Prickles, much to Sami's amazement. "I'll take that bet."

Prickles continued, "Let's all make our way back to the top and try again, with you giving us a ten-second head start. If we win, Sami goes without lunch, and if you win, Spike and I go without lunch."

Spike was just about to say something, as he was very hungry and didn't fancy missing out on his lunch, but chose to stay quiet and trust Prickles once again.

Soon they were at the top getting ready when Spike whispered to Prickles, "What's the plan then?"

"Simple," Prickles whispered back, making sure the others couldn't hear her, "when they say go, lean forward and curl up into a ball. We will roll down into the hill so fast Sami will never catch us."

"Brilliant," Spike whispered back, "looks like I will be having lunch after all, you clever, clever girl."

"Ready, steady, go," shouted Sami with a smug smile on his face, which was soon wiped away when he saw the hedgehogs lean forward, curl up into ball and roll down the slope.

"No," he shouted after them, "that's not fair," and immediately started running without even waiting for the ten-second head start he promised them. Rosie, Ricky and Stan all followed him, but, despite running as fast as they could, they soon realised none of them stood any chance of catching the fast-rolling hedgehogs.

By the time Spike and Prickles finally stopped, their heads were spinning with dizziness and they kept falling over every time they tried to stand up, but they were laughing at the same time, especially watching Sami stomp around in anger.

"Very clever," exclaimed Sami, "but you cheated, so it doesn't count."

"No, we didn't," said Prickles, "we won fair and square. We just used our spines rather than our feet."

Sami was not happy, especially now he would have to miss his lunch, but quickly calmed down when Prickles agreed to forget the bet, and he soon joined the others in praising Prickles for such a clever plan.

"Rolling will be our new game from now on," said Spike, "but I can't do it too many times, it makes me very dizzy," he explained. They all laughed and decided to climb back up the top and enjoy a well-earned lunch, followed by a short rest before a few more races.

Prickles made up a new song:

> *Rolling and racing as fast as we know*
> *From top to bottom never going slow*
> *Faster and faster we must go*
> *Beating the others is what I know.*

Later in the afternoon, Prickles was fed up with getting dizzy, so came up with another great idea, using a piece of bark to sit on and slide down the slope. Soon, she and Spike had found the right size piece of bark and tied vines to them to hold onto as they slid down the slope, which was just as fast as rolling, but without the dizziness.

Prickles named it 'hedging', which was a combination of hedgehog and sliding, but Spike came up with 'sledging', which they all agreed was an even better name.

The afternoon was great fun and time flew by, but after the sixth race Stan said, "Come on everyone, we need to be getting back in time for dinner," and they quickly set off, keen to be back before sunset. As they were coming down the hill, Stan spotted something in the distance.

"Look," Stan said, pointing towards Southwood at what appeared to be an army of yellow machines. "What on earth are they?"

Chapter Three

A Forest Divided

The six friends stood in silence looking towards the yellow machines in the distance, sensing they brought danger, but not understanding why.

"Let's go," said Stan, "maybe our parents will be able to explain," and they carried on back to Oakwood.

It wasn't long before they arrived at the fallen Great Oak Tree where their parents were waiting for them to have dinner.

"Did you have fun?" said Belle, Rosie's mother.

"We did," said Stan, "but what are those yellow machines we saw in Southwood?" wondering why the parents hadn't mentioned them first.

"Don't worry," said his father, "they are probably here to remove the Great Oak Tree."

They were very relieved with the explanation, which made perfect sense, although a little sad that the king of the forest and their favourite hide and seek spot would be taken away forever.

They sat and chatted while enjoying their dinner, explaining to their parents about their great day at the short hill, talking excitedly about how Spike and Prickles had beat Sami by rolling and how they then invented 'sledging.' Prickles' father, Pop, laughed when they talked about the bet with Sami and was even more impressed when he heard about her idea to slide down on pieces of bark. He wrapped his arms around her saying, "You really are the cleverest little hedgehog," and gave her a big kiss. All the other parents agreed and congratulated Prickles for inventing yet another game the youngsters could play.

Spike's father, Henry, was sitting there thinking, very concerned about the machines. "The machines are currently in Southwood, but they will move up here soon," he said. "We will need to make sure we are safe and well away from them when they remove the tree. I suggest that instead of meeting here at the Great Oak Tree, we meet at Hollow Pond in future, which is only ten minutes further north."

"Good idea," said Pop, "does everyone agree?"

Everyone nodded their heads in agreement.

<hr />

As planned, they met at Hollow Pond every morning, where the six youngsters would go off and play, while the adults spent time gathering food: slugs, worms and insects for the hedgehogs; wildflowers, grass and plants for the rabbits; and nuts, seeds, fruit and insects for the squirrels.

They always gathered together for dinner and often lunch, with the youngsters sharing news of their games and adventures. Trips to the short hill for 'sledging' were more and more common. Life in Oakwood Forest was better than any young animal could ever hope for. The only disturbance was the noise of the machines, which seemed to get louder every day.

After dinner one evening, the youngsters went to play a final game of hide and seek before bedtime, while the adults gathered together and talked about the machines.

"There is something wrong," said Syd, the squirrels' father. "Saffi and I climbed up in the trees today and went all the way down into Southwood. The machines are making a wide path, much wider than needed to remove the Great Oak Tree and it goes on for ever, much further than we've ever travelled. What do you think they are doing?" he asked the others.

"I don't know," said Pippa, "but if they come any further north, we are going to have to move home," she said, rather worriedly.

"Listen," said Pop, "we are all guessing what is happening, but none of us really know, so let's just keep a close watch and keep each other updated on what we see and hear."

It was only two days later that it happened. The machines finally arrived at Oakwood, making a path wider than any of them had ever seen before. This left Pippa and Pop with no choice but to quickly move out of their home before it was destroyed. With so little time, the hedgehogs decided to move into Eastwood, closer to where their squirrel friends lived. Prickles didn't want to leave her lovely home, but at the same time asked why they couldn't go and live near Spike.

"Listen, little one," said Pop in a soft voice, "I know it's difficult to leave our lovely home, but the most important thing is to collect our possessions and move them to somewhere close by and safe. It will take us all night just to move to Eastwood, whereas travelling up to Hilltop, where Spike lives, will take even longer, especially going backwards and forwards with our belongings."

Prickles wasn't happy, but accepted what her father said and helped pack things up ready for the move. Stan, Sami and their parents came to help and it wasn't until the early hours of the morning that they finally finished, with everyone falling into a deep sleep.

The hedgehogs didn't wake up until the next afternoon and only then because Sami and Stan were shouting into their burrow. "It's the machines!" blurted out Sami, as Pickles appeared.

"What's happened?" said Prickles, worriedly.

"It's the path," said Sami, panicking. "The machines have removed the Great Oak Tree and are now making the path go through Oakwood and up into Northwood."

"What?" said Prickles, panicking, "how have they come so quickly and why haven't they stopped?"

"I don't know," said Sami, "but it must have happened while we were all asleep."

"Mum, Dad, quickly we must go and look," exclaimed Prickles, but it was obvious her father was not going anywhere.

"Not until the machines have stopped for the day," he said, "it's far too dangerous for us."

Prickles knew he was right and within a couple of hours the banging and crashing of the machines stopped, so they went as fast as they could back towards the centre of Oakwood.

They looked in horror at what they saw. The machines had made a deep wide channel right through the centre of Oakwood. It came from Southwood and went right up into Northwood, splitting the forest in two.

"How will we ever get across?" cried Prickles, with tears flooding down her cheeks.

"We cannot cross it at the moment," said Pop, "it's too deep and too dangerous. Climbing down into the channel would be difficult, but getting out on the other side almost impossible. If we went in and couldn't get out before the machines come back tomorrow, we would be killed and we cannot take that risk."

They stood watching the path for a long time before turning around and walking slowly back to Eastwood. Prickles cried all the way back to her new home. Why is this happening to her lovely forest? she thought.

Spike, as you can imagine, was furious. The day after Prickles and her parents moved to a new home, they didn't appear at Hollow Pond. On that very same day the machines came, louder than ever before and driving a path right through Oakwood, separating Eastwood from Westwood for the first time. Late in the day when the machines had stopped, Spike begged his father to let him cross the path and find Prickles, but he refused.

"Listen, son," said Henry, "the path is too deep for you to get out on the other side and, even if you did, how would Prickles and her parents be able to climb out on this side?"

Spike didn't have the answer. It slowly dawned on him that he would have to wait for the machines to finish before he stood any chance of being reunited with his friends. How long would that be, he wondered?

Days turned into weeks and weeks turned into months, with the machines going up and down the massive path they had created, making it longer, wider and deeper than ever before.

Spike was fortunate because he still had Rosie and Ricky to play with, but life just wasn't the same without Prickles and, of course, Sami and Stan. It was the same for Prickles. She had the twin squirrels who were brilliant at keeping her spirits up and great fun to play with, but she missed her other friends, especially Spike, and longed for the day when all six of them could be together again.

Autumn came and went, with the forest floor now a carpet of red and golden fallen leaves. Before they knew it, winter was around the corner, bringing much shorter days and frosty nights, which meant it was now time for the hedgehogs to hibernate and sleep during the cold months.

Both hedgehog families went to sleep around the same time, looking forward to waking up in spring, hoping that the machines would have left the forest forever and they could all be reunited.

The winter months were cold and often snowy which slowed down work on the path, but, despite this, the machines kept working while the hedgehogs slept. The machines finally finished their work in early spring, just as the flowers started to peep through the carpet of leaves and the hedgehogs started to wake from their hibernation.

Prickles' parents woke her up slowly, and they had a lovely meal of fresh worms that her father had gathered earlier. As soon as they were finished, they left their home in Eastwood and rushed to see if the machines had left and, if so, what they had left behind.

As they arrived in Oakwood, they were amazed to discover the deep wide channel was now a wide black path, level with the forest floor, with white broken lines along it. The path went from Southwood to Northwood as far as the eye could see.

"What is it?" asked Prickles.
"I have no idea," said her mother, "but it doesn't look like it was built for animals."

They stood there for a while not knowing what to do when Stan, Sami and their parents, Saffi and Syd, arrived.

"We heard you were awake," said Sami, and they started to hug, pleased to see each other after the long hibernation.
"Do you know what this is?" asked Prickles to the squirrels, pointing at the black path. "It's a road," said Syd, in a solemn voice.
"What's a road?" asked Prickles.
"It's something humans use to travel in fast machines called cars," said Syd. "They are very fast, very dangerous and noisy too," he continued. "There has never been a road anywhere near the forest before and now we have one right through the middle."

Just as he finished his sentence, they heard a loud rumbling sound coming towards them.

"What's that noise?" screamed Prickles, as they ran back from the road.

Before anyone could answer her, it happened. Hundreds of cars started to whizz past them, travelling in both directions, while the animals just stared at them, frozen in fear.

They quickly retreated to Eastwood when Prickles stopped and turned to Pop, "How are we going to get across the road to see Spike, Rosie and Ricky?" she asked with tears streaming down her face.

Pop knelt down in front of her, and replied, "I'm sorry little one, we won't be able to cross the road, it's far too dangerous."

Prickles just stood there looking at her mother and father, shaking her head, trying to make sense of what she had just been told. She walked back home, struggling to stop the tears, realising that if she had woken up sooner, they might have been able to cross the road. Now, she would never see Spike, Rosie and Ricky again.

A few days later on the other side of the road, Spike woke from his hibernation, but this time to what sounded like constant hum coming from the bottom of the hill. He didn't wait for his parents, but ran straight out to see what was making the noise. He met Rosie and Ricky on the way, who began to tell him about the new road, humans and cars, but he wasn't really listening. He just wanted to see what was happening for himself.

When he arrived, he couldn't believe his eyes. Hundreds of different types of vehicles were racing up and down. He realised immediately that no animal could ever cross that road and get to the other side alive, especially a slow hedgehog.

Rosie and Ricky tried to console him, just as Sami and Stan had tried to console Prickles, but both hedgehogs were heartbroken having woken from their hibernation full of hope, only to discover they had woken up too late.

Spike stood there in shock. Would he ever see Prickles again?

Chapter Four

Ricky's Lucky Find

The animals on both sides of the road were feeling so sad, realising that now that humans were travelling along the road in such fast vehicles, they might never see their friends again.

The squirrels' and rabbits' parents had made them promise to never try to cross the road. They were worried that their youngsters might try to help Spike and Prickles, but it was clear they all realised the dangers of the new road.

Prickles was angry. She could always come up with a plan, yet no matter how hard she tried, she couldn't think of a safe way to get across the road. While she and Spike were both devastated, surprisingly it was Rosie who was suffering the most. She loved playing with Prickles, Sami and Stan every day and just couldn't imagine life without them. No matter what Ricky or Spike did to try and cheer her up, it didn't work and she transformed from being a very happy, bouncy rabbit into one that was constantly sad. Ricky felt for her, hating the humans who had built the road and ruined their lives. It made him determined to find a way to bring them all back together.

They were sitting down to dinner one evening, when Ricky spoke of a plan he had been considering.

"Listen, we can't just give up," he said. "Somewhere, somehow there is a way to get across the road, it's just not here."

"What are you suggesting?" said Roger, starting to worry about what his son was about to propose.

"I am young and I am fast," said Ricky. "I'm going to follow the road back down into Southwood to find somewhere to cross. After all, it must start somewhere and that somewhere may be the place to cross."

They all looked at each other waiting for someone to speak, and Rosie's eyes filled with tears of happiness, knowing he was doing this for her.

"Okay," said Roger, "but you may travel for three days only. If you haven't found any way across by then, you must turn back. The longest you should be gone is six days. Agreed?"

Ricky nodded and went to hug both his parents and then Rosie.

"I'll leave first thing tomorrow," Ricky said, determined to bring all the friends back together.

Rosie couldn't sleep. She was really worried. She had already lost her Eastwood friends and now the person she cared for the most in the world, Ricky, was going on a dangerous mission just for her. She couldn't bear the thought of losing him too. I must stop him, she thought, and was waiting outside his warren when he came out early in the morning, having just said goodbye to his parents. She threw her arms around him, tears running down her face and said, "Please don't go, I'm scared you won't come back."

Ricky held her closely and whispered, "Listen, I will be back and I will find a way across, remember I miss them as much as you."

Ricky continued, "I can outrun most animals in this forest, so you've got nothing to worry about, just trust me and be here for Spike and our parents."

She smiled to herself, realising she was not going to change his mind and gave him a big hug, while whispering good luck before kissing him goodbye. She waved frantically as he darted off along the side of the road, tears of happiness and pride running down her face.

Ricky followed the road until midday, when he decided to stop for lunch. He stopped by a stream where he took a long drink, before gathering some weeds and wildflowers, which he enjoyed as he took a well-earned rest. He was tired, but felt he had made good progress, even though he hadn't seen any sign of somewhere safe to cross.

After a short rest, he decided to carry on travelling south, and did so until the spring sun began to set and he realised his legs couldn't carry him any further. He decided to go a little way into the forest, away from the road, and dig a small hole to sleep in, before gathering some food for dinner. He soon fell asleep. A whole day of travelling had made him very weary.

Ricky woke at sunrise the following day and was surprised at how much his legs ached. He had obviously pushed himself too much on day one and realised he had to pace himself better on day two, otherwise he wouldn't be able to walk at all by day three.

He made his way back to the road and set off at a much steadier pace, stopping after two hours for a short rest, followed by another two hours, then lunch. He did the same in the afternoon, with two rest stops, before finally calling it a day and stopping for dinner and sleep.

As he lay in the shallow hole he had dug, he was starting to get worried. He had now travelled for two long days and there was no sign of anywhere to cross or the road coming to an end. He only had one more day to go before he promised his father he would turn back.

He woke on the third morning, just as the sun started to warm his bed, full of hope that today he would find somewhere safe to cross the road. It was going to be a good day, he decided, and set off on his travels, continuing to look for that safe crossing place.

Again, he stopped every two hours, but this time travelled six hours before lunch and another six hours after lunch, not wanting the day to end, but as darkness fell, he realised he had run out of time.

He gathered some food and sat down to eat, sad that he hadn't found a way to cross the road. One more hour, he thought to himself, then I'll call it quits.

Despite his tired legs, he got up and pushed forward, praying that he would find something. Just as he was getting to the point where his legs would carry him no further, he found himself at a large lake, signposted Willow Waters. In moonlight he could see the willow trees with their lower branches and leaves hanging into the water, giving the lake its name.

He made the difficult decision to stop there for the night, having given up any hope of finding a safe way across the road. Despite travelling miles and miles, the road appeared to go on forever. He was dreading the journey back home, especially knowing he would have to tell Spike and Rosie that there was no hope of ever reaching the others.

It was now dark and he was very tired so he started to dig a hole to sleep in. It was as he was digging that something strange happened – he hit something very hard. Why would there be something hard in the ground near a lake? he thought.

He decided to investigate, and, although it was difficult to see, he noticed something very strange. The lake had an overflow that fed into a big square tunnel that went all the way under the road.
Ricky couldn't hold back his excitement and started jumping up and down, so pleased with his lucky find. He may have finally found a way to cross the road, which even in the dark had cars speeding along it, headlights blazing ahead of them.

He jumped down into the tunnel, which had a trickle of water flowing through it, and slowly walked under the road until he reached the other side. It was there he discovered that the tunnel fed another smaller lake on the other side of the road, which was signposted Willow Pond.

Because the tunnel has a sloping exit, he could easily step out of it and onto the grass banks of Willow Pond.

He was so excited and pleased that he had found a way across, he decided to make his burrow on the banks of Willow Pond and sleep in Eastwood that night. He would cross back and set off for home in the morning. He couldn't wait to tell Spike and Rosie the great news.

Ricky dug a small hole at the base of a tree, crawled in and immediately went straight to sleep, dreaming of how excited Spike and Rosie would be. He woke up early the next morning and was surprised to see that it had been raining overnight and everything was wet. He must have been so tired he had slept right through it.

He walked along the edge of Willow Pond to the tunnel and gasped. The tunnel was now full of running water, stopping him from crossing back. He held his head in his paws. What had happened? he thought. Why did the tunnel have so much water and how was he going to get back across?

After a while he realised that the overnight rain had caused the water level in Willow Waters to rise, which caused it to overflow into the tunnel and flow into Willow Pond.

Ricky was in despair. He had no idea how long it would take for Willow Waters to stop overflowing, or if there was any more rain due. He could be stuck there for days until the water level in the tunnel dropped.

He thought long and hard. Should he wait or should he go and find Stan, Sami, Prickles and their parents, and bring them back to the tunnel? Hopefully, by the time he collected them and got them back to the tunnel, the water levels would have dropped and they could all cross safely.

Finding them, telling them about the tunnel and bringing them back would take days and mean he would break his promise to return in six days, but what choice did he have? With the very deep water in the tunnel, he couldn't get back anyway.

Ricky was happy with his new plan, so he set off with a spring in his step, excited about the thought of seeing his friends again, bringing them back to tunnel and finally reuniting them all.

It took three long days, following the road north, before Ricky finally reached Oakwood, where the Great Oak Tree used to be. It took him a little time to search, before he finally found his long-lost friends, who were having dinner.

Sami saw him first, 'Ricky!' he shouted, leaping up and running quickly towards him.

The others couldn't believe their eyes. Prickles burst into tears of happiness as she ran up and hugged him, refusing to let go.

Prickles, Stan, Sami and their parents all had a million questions for him about Spike, Rosie, their parents, and life in Westwood and Hilltop.

He answered them as fast as he could, before they all sat down and listened to the most important part of all, his journey and how he crossed the road. They couldn't believe he had been travelling for six whole days and were amazed when he shared his story of his 'lucky find', the tunnel.

He then went on to tell them about the overnight rain, which caused the tunnel to flood, and how he decided to come and get them rather than waiting for it to dry out and go back.

He was their hero and they could not stop thanking him, until Pop finally noticed how tired he was and suggested they all go to bed to let Ricky get a good night's sleep. They could carry on the conversation in the morning and start to plan their journey.

"Goodnight Ricky, love you," called Prickles as she headed off with her parents to their burrow.
"Fantastic to see you, Ricky," shouted Sami.
"Thank you, Ricky," shouted Stan, as he made his way with Sami back up into the trees.

Ricky smiled to himself, so pleased that they were all so happy and couldn't wait to get them all safely back to Westwood, especially to see the expressions on Spike and Rosie's faces.

Prickles went to bed that night happier than she could ever remember. Finally, she would be reunited with Spike, and of course Rosie and their families. She couldn't get to sleep, so excited that they would soon be making plans to travel to Hilltop. Eventually, she did fall asleep and dreamed about the six of them playing hide and seek and 'sledging' down hills. It was the best dream she'd had in a long, long time.

It was a beautiful morning. The sun was shining, the trees were in full leaf and the birds were singing as they gathered food for a big celebration breakfast. They had woken up early and gathered Ricky's favourite food of fresh grass and berries, which they carefully laid out for him.

Ricky finally woke and, although he was still exhausted from his travels, joined them and tucked into the best breakfast ever. It wasn't long before they were making plans for the return journey.

While Sami was the playful one, he was also wise like his father and always thinking ahead.

"We will need to be very careful when travelling," Sami said to the others. "It's okay for us squirrels and Ricky, as we are all fast and can outrun most of the dangers, but it's different for the hedgehogs."
He went on, "We need to be on the look-out for foxes and badgers."

"I suggest Stan and I travel up in the trees, checking everything is clear up ahead. Mum, Dad and Ricky should travel with Prickles, Pippa and Pop, keeping an eye out at ground level," he continued.

"Excellent idea," said the twins' father proudly. "I suggest we leave first thing tomorrow morning, after another hearty breakfast, as it sounds like we have a long way to go."
Everyone agreed and, while it was going to be difficult to leave their lovely homes in Eastwood, they couldn't wait to be reunited with their lifelong friends.

Meanwhile, back in Westwood, Rosie was inconsolable. Ricky had not returned after the six days as agreed, and as more days passed by, even his parents started to fear they had lost their beloved son for ever.

Chapter Five

Prickles saves the Day

It was an early start but after breakfast they were all raring to go. "Come on then, let's get going and we will soon be able to see our friends," said Ricky proudly, taking charge as he led the way, ahead of Prickles and her parents.

As planned, Sami and Stan were high up in the trees, keeping lookout. They travelled for two hours, before stopping for a rest, then another two hours, before stopping for well-deserved lunch. In the afternoon they travelled for another four long hours, before stopping for the day.

Prickles and her parents, Pop and Pippa, were absolutely exhausted. Their little legs had never walked so far. Pippa and Pop were constantly worried about foxes and badgers, so after dinner they found a suitable place to make a shallow nest where they could sleep safely, with the others close by.

The journey to Willow Pond was slow, long and very tiring, but fortunately uneventful, and it was as the sun started to set on the sixth day of travelling they finally saw the glistening waters.

Prickles was so excited she began to sing:

We've reached the pond and soon the lake
Seeing Spike and Rosie will be just great
We've travelled so far and for so long
I couldn't be happier singing this song.

The others joined in with the singing and Ricky had the biggest smile on his face, pleased it was he who discovered the tunnel and was now leading them back to their friends.

Just as Ricky had hoped, the water flowing into the tunnel from Willow Waters was just a trickle, which made him determined to cross that evening in case it rained overnight and flooded again. After they had rested for a little while, Ricky said excitedly, "Come on everyone, it's time to cross into Westwood," and within no time at all they were lining up next to the tunnel's slope.

Sami and Stan helped the hedgehogs down the steep slope, and Ricky led the animals along the dark tunnel towards Willow Waters.

The hedgehogs were scared of the noise in the tunnel, which came from the cars zooming up and down the road above their heads but were still eager to cross.

"It's louder than the thunder of the Great Storm," shouted Prickles, as loud as she could.

As they reached the far side of the tunnel Ricky suddenly realised they had a huge problem. He had jumped down from Willow Waters into the tunnel and, while rabbits and squirrels could use their springy back legs to jump out, the hedgehogs couldn't. The group stood looking at the wall in silence, trying frantically to think of a way to help the hedgehogs climb out.

"Listen," said Sami, breaking the awkward silence. "We will figure out a way to climb the wall, but it's getting late. Why don't we go back to Willow Pond, have dinner and get a good night's sleep and work out a plan in the morning?"

They all reluctantly nodded in agreement and made their way back, finding a safe place in the roots of a large willow tree, where they ate and slept huddled together for safety.

Poor Ricky didn't sleep well at all. He was so disappointed and upset that he had brought them all this way, raising their hopes of a reunion with their friends, but, stupidly, hadn't thought about how the hedgehogs would climb the tunnel wall. There must be a way, he thought, but no matter how hard he tried, he couldn't work out a plan.

Prickles was the same. She couldn't sleep either and kept thinking of ways they could scale the tunnel wall. Like Ricky, she was struggling to come up with a solution and her mind started to wander, thinking about all the fun she used to have playing with the rabbits, squirrels and, most of all, her best friend, Spike. She pictured them playing hide and seek, singing her song:

Hide and seek is so much fun
I'll soon find you one by one
I will look under roots and behind the trees
There is no way of hiding from me.

She also thought about the time when she raced Sami down the short hill, by curling up and rolling down the slope, when suddenly she sat up. That's it, she thought, we can curl up and roll!

It was still the middle of the night when she woke the others.

"Wake up, wake up, I have a plan!" she shouted excitedly.

Ricky was up first as he was struggling to sleep anyway and soon the others had gathered round, tired, but excited to hear Prickles' idea.

She explained to them how she was remembering the fun times they used to have playing hide and seek and racing down the short hill, when she realised that rolling was the solution to their problem.

Ricky looked at her, totally confused. "You and Spike used to roll down the hill," he said. "What has that got to do with getting out of a tunnel?", shaking his head to show that he still didn't understand.

"Instead of rolling down, you are going help us hedgehogs roll up," she said, excitedly.

Ricky was still confused. Prickles smiled at him, realising that she hadn't explained her plan very well.

"Ricky" she said, confidently, "you have big strong springy back legs, don't you?"
"Yes," he replied, still confused. "Well, imagine if you lay on your back with your back feet against the wall of the tunnel," Prickles continued, as she started to explain her plan. "If we climb up onto the underside

of your feet and roll up into a ball, you can then kick your legs as hard as you can, sending us spinning up into the air and over the edge of the tunnel wall. We will land on the grass bank and our spines will help soften the landing. The squirrels could be up on the grass bank to make sure we have a safe landing." She looked at everyone for approval, pleased with herself for coming up with such a good plan.

Everyone stood in silence, trying to picture in their minds what Prickles had described. Was it a crazy idea that wouldn't work, or a brilliant plan that was bound to succeed? Pop figured it out pretty quickly and could picture exactly what she had suggested. He started to smile, quickly realising that his daughter really was a genius.

"Fantastic idea!" shouted Pop, "I love it! Ricky, are you up for giving it a go?"
"Certainly," said Ricky, feeling a great relief that someone had come up with a plan where he couldn't, and even better that it needed his help to succeed.

Pippa wasn't so keen, especially the thought of being 'spun up into the air', but Prickles quickly explained that she didn't hurt herself when she rolled down the short hill as her spines acted like springs.

They all agreed it was worth a try, before Pop said, "Okay, but let's all get a few more hours' sleep and try it first thing in the morning. It's still far too early and we need our sleep if we are going to travel a full day tomorrow."

They all agreed and went back to the large willow tree. At last, Prickles and Ricky could sleep soundly knowing that there was a plan that might just work.

They awoke just as the sun started to rise and, without delay, went to the tunnel to try out Prickles' plan. Breakfast would have to wait.

Once again, they walked under the noisy road. The squirrels jumped up the tunnel wall to make sure they picked a place with a nice soft grass landing. Sami called down to Ricky and told him where to position himself, lying down in a puddle, legs up against the wall.

Prickles volunteered to go first as it was her idea. She climbed up onto Ricky, then up onto the underside of his feet and gave everyone a thumbs up, before she curled up into a ball with her back resting between the underside of his feet and the tunnel wall.

Ricky found the spines tickled his feet and he struggled to keep them still, but his role was too important to mess up now through tickly feet.

"Ready when you are," said Prickles, with a slight tremble in her voice, feeling nervous now that the plan was about to become reality.
"Okay," said Ricky, "I'm going to count to three, then push."

The others were watching, excited to see if her plan would work, all except Pippa, who just closed her eyes and covered them with her paws.

"One, two, three!" shouted Ricky, before pushing his springy back legs as fast and hard as he could, catapulting Prickles up into the air and spinning as she flew high above the tunnel wall before disappearing out of sight.

Ricky realised immediately that he had pushed her far too hard and quickly jumped up the tunnel wall in time to see her come bouncing down on the grass, rolling with Sami and Stan chasing frantically after her, until she finally stopped, hitting the bottom of a small tree.

They all ran over and were relieved when she uncurled herself and gave out a massive yell of excitement.

"Yes, yes!" Prickles shouted, "it worked!". She gave Ricky, Sami and Stan a massive hug, pleased that her plan was a success.

"Quick, let's get Mum and Dad up here," she said, as they all ran back to the tunnel and leaned over, giving a big thumbs up to the parents, who were waiting in anticipation. The parents jumped for joy, smiling with happiness at the success of Pickles' idea.

Ricky climbed back down, and they agreed Pippa was next, but this time Ricky promised not to push quite so hard. Nervously, Pippa climbed up and curled up into a ball on his feet, trembling as she said "ready." Without waiting, Ricky shouted, "One, two, three, go!" and pushed his rear legs upwards, but nowhere near as hard or fast this time. Up she flew, spinning just like Prickles, but not so high, coming down safely on the soft grass with only a small bounce and a short roll.

Prickles rushed up to her and gave her a big hug as she uncurled herself, smiling at her first, and hopefully last flying roll.

They both rushed up to the tunnel wall and gave the thumbs up for Pop's turn.

Soon the animals were congratulating Prickles for her brilliant plan and Ricky for his perfect launching. The adults went off in search of food for breakfast, while Prickles talked with Stan, Sami and Ricky about how much fun it was spinning in the air, with Sami demanding he got to have a go next time.

After the adults returned and they finished eating, Ricky said, "Come on everyone, we've got a long way to travel" and they were soon on their way.

Prickles started to sing:

> We've reached the pond and now the lake
> Seeing Spike and Rosie will just be great
> We've travelled so far and so long
> I couldn't be happier singing this song.

They all joined in and sang together as they walked along, following the road towards Northwood:

> We've reached the pond and now the lake
> Seeing Spike and Rosie will just be great
> We've travelled so far and so long
> We couldn't be happier singing this song.

By now, it had been thirteen days since Ricky had set off, leaving Spike, Rosie and their families in Westwood now fearing the worst.

Prickles, Stan, Sami and Ricky were in such a happy and jovial mood as they got closer to the long-awaited reunion, but they had no idea of the dangers that lay ahead.

Chapter Six

Daisy and Dexter to the Rescue

They had just sat down for dinner at the end of the fifth day of travelling since crossing the tunnel. It was eleven days since they left Eastwood and eighteen days since Ricky had left Westwood. Only one more day to go, thought Ricky, pleased at the speed they were making. The hedgehogs were slow, he thought, but they are doing well, and everyone's spirits were high, knowing that they were nearly at the end of their journey and they would soon be reunited with their friends. Finally, he would see his beloved Rosie again.

Over dinner, Prickles was so excited about the progress they were making that she kept talking louder and louder.

"I can't wait to see Spike," she said excitedly. "Can you imagine the look on his face when he sees us all?" Speaking to Ricky, she said, "What about Rosie and your parents? They will be so relieved. I also can't wait for us all to play hide and seek together again," she said and started singing her song:

> Hide and seek is so much fun
> I'll soon find you one by one
> I will look under roots and behind the trees
> There is no way you're hiding from me.

"Quietly, Prickles," said her father, Pop, "you're being far too loud. You must remember there are lots of dangers out there and we don't want to let them know we are here."

"Sorry, Dad," said Prickles, feeling embarrassed that she had got herself over excited.

"Don't worry, little one," he said, "just talk quietly in future," and they continued to talk about how exciting it would be to see all their friends, while they finished their meal.

Unknown to them all, Prickles' voice had been a little too loud and it carried a long way in the quiet forest. Unfortunately, it carried all the way to the den of two foxes, Freddie and Fergie, whose ears pricked up when they heard the sound of her singing.

"Yummy," said Freddie, licking his lips as he looked Fergie, "I hear dinner calling."

Fergie smiled and licked her lips, too, and they hurriedly set off in the direction of the squeaky little voice.

After dinner, Prickles, Stan, Sami and Ricky played hide and seek as there was still enough light, even though the sun had started to set.

"Be careful and don't go too far," said Pippa.

Stan, Sami and Ricky hid first, while Prickles counted to thirty.

"Coming, ready or not," she called and quietly sang her song as she looked for the others:

> *Hide and seek is so much fun*
> *I'll soon find you one by one*
> *I will look under roots and behind the trees*
> *There is no way of hiding from me.*

Even though she was singing quietly, Prickles' song was leading the foxes straight to her.

It wasn't long before Prickles found Stan. She then started looking for Sami and Ricky, and, as she was sneaking her way behind a large fir tree, she looked up and saw the two foxes blocking her path. She didn't have the time or the speed to run, but fortunately remembered what her parents had told her to do when in trouble. She curled up into a ball and used her spines to protect her.

Stan saw what was happening and called out to Sami and Ricky for help. The foxes ran up to Prickles and started to kick her with their paws, trying to make her uncurl so they could get to her soft underbelly. Stan could see what they were doing and, desperate to help her, ran and jumped onto Freddie's back, digging in his claws, hoping to distract him from attacking Prickles.

Sami and Ricky heard Stan's cries and dashed out of their hiding place, just in time to see Stan jumping onto Freddie's back and Prickles curled up into a ball between the two foxes.

Without hesitating or thinking about his own safety, Sami did the same as Stan and jumped onto Fergie's back.

With the foxes distracted, trying to shake off the squirrels clinging onto their backs, Ricky saw an opportunity to get Prickles to safety. He ran up to her, and, while she was still curled up in a ball, rolled her along the ground and around the back of a big oak tree.

He frantically dug a shallow hole and rolled her in it, before covering her up with the loose earth.

"Lie here quietly and don't move until I come back," he whispered.

Until he spoke, Prickles had no idea what was happening and was trembling with fear, but felt some relief when she heard Ricky's voice.

Ricky ran back to see how the squirrels were doing, just as Fergie managed to shake Sami off, catapulting him into the air. Sami landed and ran up a nearby tree, considering his next move.

Stan was still clinging onto Freddie when suddenly he saw Fergie come running up towards Freddie. Fergie jumped up, knocking Stan off Freddie's back with her legs. Stan fell badly, knocking himself out as he landed on a tree root.

Freddie and Fergie shook themselves and immediately started to look around for Prickles, who had somehow disappeared.

They searched for a few minutes before they looked at one another and turned towards Stan.

"Oh well," said Freddie, "it looks like it's squirrel for dinner rather than hedgehog," which made Fergie laugh out loud.

They moved slowly towards Stan who was lying on the ground, motionless. Ricky and Sami were both ready to pounce and protect Stan, when suddenly there was a movement coming from the bushes to the side of them. Within seconds, two large deer came crashing through the bushes and charged towards the foxes. The larger deer, with a splendid set of antlers, lowered his head as he charged straight into the unsuspecting foxes, sending them flying into the air, before they came tumbling down along the forest floor.

The foxes looked up and saw the second, smaller but equally powerful deer, charging towards them. Fergie managed to jump out of the way, but Freddie wasn't so quick and again found himself hit side-on and launched into the air. He landed hard, with a terrible pain in his ribs, but still managed to get up quickly, determined to avoid another attack.

With both deer now chasing after them, Fergie and Freddie ran deep into the forest, as fast as they could, until they saw the deer stop and turn back towards the road.

Sami ran to see if Stan was alright, while Ricky went to retrieve Prickles from her hiding place. By now, all the parents had arrived having heard all the noise and commotion. Ricky managed to convince Prickles that it was safe to come out and she slowly uncurled herself and shook off all the earth.

"What happened to the foxes?" Prickles asked nervously, and Ricky quickly explained everything as they made their way back to see Stan.

Sami had Stan's head on his lap while all the others were gathered around in silence, but fortunately it wasn't long before he started to stir, holding his head as he woke up.

"Ouch, that hurt my head," Stan said with a cheeky grin on his face, making Sami laugh in relief.
"Prickles, you're okay!" Stan said in amazement, seeing her brush off the dirt from her spines, "but what happened to the foxes?"

At the same time, the two deer who had saved them appeared from the trees. It was Dexter and Daisy. Daisy said, "It's okay everyone, you're safe now, but I think we should stay with you tonight, just to make sure Freddie and Fergie don't return. After all, they are probably very angry that they missed out on their dinner."

The parents were horrified to hear about the fox attack, but proud of how Stan, Sami and Ricky had tried to protect Prickles.

They couldn't thank Daisy and Dexter enough for undoubtedly saving Stan's life. Prickles couldn't believe what her friends had done to help save her, or how lucky Stan had been that the deer had arrived just in the nick of time.

The deer escorted them back to where they had earlier eaten dinner. They found somewhere close by to sleep for the night, promising to stay on guard so that the smaller animals could rest safely.

Everyone woke the next morning in great spirits. Daisy and Dexter were amazed as the animals told their story of how the new road had separated them from their friends, how Ricky had travelled to find a way across the road and how they 'spun' out of the tunnel.

The deer were so impressed and keen to see them all get back safely to their friends, especially Spike who they knew already, that they suggested they travel with the group, just in case the foxes wanted revenge for the previous night's failed attempt.

They finished breakfast and set off again, this time not stopping to rest. Everyone was so excited about the prospect of seeing their friends again and being able to tell them about the adventures they had encountered during their journey.

It was nineteen days since Ricky had set off to find a way across the busy road. Rosie and Spike had given up any hope of him ever returning.

Spike was wandering alone around Hilltop, thinking about Ricky, Sami and Stan, and, of course, Prickles. He smiled every time he thought about his clever little friend, remembering all the games she invented and the songs she made up for each of them. His favourite was the original song, which she sang before they met their other friends:

> *Hide and seek is so much fun*
> *I'll soon find you my little Spikey one*
> *I will look under roots and behind the trees*
> *There is no way of hiding from me.*

He was singing the song quietly and was just about to make his way back home, when he imagined that he could hear Prickles singing it too. He carried on singing but started shaking his head to try to get the sound of her voice to stop as it was making him upset, but it wouldn't go away.

He suddenly stopped singing, yet could still hear her lovely voice behind him. Just then, he turned around to see Prickles stepping out from behind a large tree, singing at the top of her voice.

Prickles ran towards him and he ran to meet her, feeling a happiness like he had never experienced before. They kissed and hugged, not saying a word, just content at holding each other. It had been a long, long time.

Then, from behind the same tree, came Sami and Stan, followed by all their parents. Just when Spike thought he couldn't have been any happier, Ricky appeared. Spike wept with joy at seeing his long-lost friend again.

Tears of happiness were flowing and they all hugged and cheered at the same time. Hearing all the noise, Spike's parents, Hetty and Henry, came rushing out of their home and couldn't believe their eyes as they ran up to join in the celebrations with their missing friends.

The noise travelled down the hill to where Rosie and Ricky's families lived and they too came running up the hill towards the clearing, to see what all the noise was about.

Rosie froze as she reached the top of the hill, seeing all her friends again for the first time in almost a year since the road had been built. Just then she spotted her hero, right in the middle of them all, Ricky. She fell to her knees, overwhelmed with emotion and happiness.

Ricky's parents, Ruby and Roger, saw him too and Ruby cried out his name in relief.

Ricky turned, hearing his name being called, and wriggled out of the gathering, running to hold his mother. He hugged Ruby and then knelt in front of Rosie who was still in a state of shock, holding her as close and as tight as he possibly could.

"I'm sorry," he whispered, "I had no choice but to go and get them and I promise, I'll never scare you like that again."

He continued to hold her and then slowly lifted her up to her feet and all the rabbits held paws as they walked to join the others, who were dancing up and down for joy.

Daisy and Dexter joined them, too, and for the next few hours the hedgehogs, rabbits, squirrels and deer all sat around listening to Ricky recount his adventures, explaining all that had happened since he set off many days ago.

Spike couldn't have been any prouder of Prickles, especially the clever plan to get out of the tunnel and could not stop thanking Ricky, Sami, Stan, Daisy and Dexter, for saving her life.

Ricky was Rosie's hero, now more than ever. It had been his idea to find a way across the road to reunite the friends, and he had succeeded, especially for her. She couldn't have been any happier or any prouder and, for the first night in a long, long time, went to sleep looking forward to the following morning, just like the rest of them.

Spike and Prickles agreed that they would never again be parted. The future for the two young hedgehogs was looking so much brighter now they were all reunited. However, there were undoubtedly many more adventures in Oakwood Forest still to come for Spike, Prickles and their friends...